RODEO

Contents

1 Shubble 5

2 Club Rodeo 15

3 Labyrinth 30

4 Agony 36

5 Vector, Inc. 40

6 District H 50

7 District L 55

8 Rodeo 66

9 The Virus 79

10 The New Beginning 85

Rodeo © 2012, 2020 Park Soyeon

Proofreader Christina De Paris

All right reserved. Nwo part of this publication may be reproduced or utilized in any form or by any means, electronic or mechanical, including photocopying recording, or by any information storage and retrieval system, without prior written permission from copyright holder.

Published in e-book 2012, in print 2020
ISBN 979-11-970845-1-5

www.goggasworld.com
Instagram/soyeonaaaa

1 Shubble

Prrrrr...

The engine of the hovercar started and died. The broker looked at Hyunsoo with doubt. The broker showed him secondhand hover cars uttering varied levels of special terminology. The broker knew he didn't understand a thing. It was a lot worse watching him in the driver's seat, though. Hyunsoo couldn't trust himself any more than the broker could.

"That's totally fine. You won't be driving manually." The broker was just saying because he was afraid of losing his customer. Of course, there was built-in GPS and automatic driving mode. The only time it mattered was when the power was out, and then he would have to drive manually. "When you have a passenger, the light comes up on this red button and his or her location shows up on the GPS." Hyunsoo listening and at the same time, he wasn't. Why did it have to be driving? Whatever the reason was, he didn't want to change his mind. He just hoped he wouldn't have to manually drive. It was the broker who worried about him changing his mind. The broker handed over the credit reader in a hurry.

Hyunsoo put his finger on it. The credit reader poked his finger with a very sharp needle. It disappeared with a small drop of his blood, which was enough to read his credit. The broker put his finger next to it. The machine transferred 2,000 credits from Hyunsoo's account to the broker's. The broker smiled. Hyunsoo felt a painful reality.

Hyunsoo knew the broker was Q6 at first sight. The typical jobs of Q6 involved a lot of interaction with people. Also, a wrinkled shirt was their usual look and immediately showing emotions was the most common characteristic. Hyunsoo was Q6. From today. From this moment.

There were seven levels of people in Shubble, the city Hyunsoo was living in. It was divided depending on credit level: Q1 had unlimited credit; Q2 had five billion; Q3 had two billion; Q5, which were mid-level office workers, had a billion. Q5 got 4,000 credits and their work was mainly physical labor. Q6 owned 2,000 credits and there wasn't a designated work. They had to choose whatever they had to do as they went along. Lastly, there was a hybrid.

Higher-level meant having a controllable life and less stress from people. At least the people in Shubble believed so. Talking with people was considered as low-level behavior and caused tremendous stress. It's possible to become a higher level. It depended on how much he or she respected the rules of the city. They worked very hard and followed the rules no matter what to obtain a higher level. Hyunsoo didn't feel quite right in Shubble, but in general, he followed the rules without a problem.

Hyunsoo was Q4 until yesterday. There were thirty other Q4 workers in the same room. They started at nine o'clock wearing a suit and tie. There was a glassy partition between each of the workers that created what was considered to be a private space for them. Hyunsoo wasn't different from them. After sitting in front of the computer for three hours straight, it was time for lunch. Fresh processed food was delivered to the lunch box mounted on the desk. It was chicken breast and fruit. He could choose plain, salty or spicy chicken, and a peach, banana or apple. He tried everything. It all tasted good, but there weren't enough choices.

He lived in a cell, like everybody else. There's enough space for a single bed, a desk, and for a person to stand. The small space was quite special because of Bitie. She was a hybrid pet that had the body of a butterfly with the head of a cat. She flew around him when he got back. She flew up and down looking like a parabola, as her head was too heavy. She wasn't pretty. Neither was her character. When she didn't like something she bit Hyunsoo hard. But when she heard unfamiliar sounds, she became frightened and hid behind him. He would stroke her forehead telling her everything was okay, then she was back to being proud again. In his cell, he finally felt human and he could smile at the end of a day.

One morning, while Hyunsoo was getting ready for work, he noticed she was acting unusual. She breathed heavily and her eyes were unfocused. She kept dropping her head because she couldn't handle the weight of it. She couldn't get up. It was time to go to work and she needed to see a veterinarian. The veterinarian opened at nine, which was the same time Hyunsoo had to be at work. It was level determination day. It was the one day of the year when the city was full of tension. Like always, he would stay in Q4. But to do that, nothing should happen until the very last moment when the level was decided. Anything could influence one's level. Being late to work meant losing credit. Work or Bitie?

Hyunsoo sent a message to work and decided to take Bitie to the vet. Bitie lay motionless in Hyunsoo's arms. When he arrived at a little spot for visitors, a little screen asked for credit. He quickly put his finger on the reader and answered the questions.

What animal is your pet hybridized with?
a. Cat
b. Dog
c. Elephant
d. Snake
e. Turtle

f. Butterfly

He checked a and f.

What are the symptoms of your pet?
1. Headache
2. Stomachache
3. Vomiting
4. Fever
5. Diarrhea

"Did she have a headache? Stomachache? There's nothing about breathing." He put his hand on Bitie to check if she had a fever. She didn't have diarrhea. A cold stainless steel plate popped out from the wall. *Insert your pet*. Hyunsoo didn't feel right. "I've got to see the vet." Somebody had to see her and talk to him about what was wrong. *Insert your pet*.

"Is anybody in there? Please check out my pet!" he shouted. The message blinked a few more times as if telling him to hurry. There wasn't any sign of people in the building. Hyunsoo's worried voice disappeared in the air. The cold metal plate seemed to be the only choice he had. Bitie looked frightened. She grabbed and pulled his sleeves with all the energy she had. She made holes and wrinkles on his shirt. Her desperate look broke his heart. "Everything will be okay. It will be fine." Hyunsoo's voice and gentle movement comforted Bitie. He laid her carefully on the plate. As soon as it sensed her, it took her away into the building. *Your pet has been successfully terminated.*

"NO!" Hyunsoo tried to pull back the plate from the wall. It wasn't moving at all. The building swallowed her. *The symptoms you chose are very common side effects of hybrid pets and are caused by imperfect hybridization. It eventually leads to the pet's death. We charged you 700 credits for the termination fee. Thank you.*

"Give her back to me!" Hyunsoo yelled and hit the screen hard in anger. People in nearby buildings and taxis flying by were looking at him. None of them were interested in why he was upset. None of them said a word. Their eyes were saying that he was vulgar and rude.

It was afternoon when Hyunsoo arrived at work. He bunched up his jacket and held it in one hand. His shirt and pants were wrinkled. He had gotten a few holes. They were Bitie's last marks. He undid a few buttons of his shirt. The workers in the office were typing and looking at him at the same time. Their eyes were following him, noticing a poorly dressed Q4 office worker.

As soon as Hyeonsoo sat down, message came up on his screen. *Mr. Lee wants to see you in his office.* Talking to the boss was the best or worst-case scenario, leading to either a promotion or relegation of the level. It was more likely to the latter. Promotions happened rarely, and even when they did, the transfer was quiet.

Speaking face to face must be an uncomfortable task for Mr. Lee. He was very close to becoming Q3 but was still Q4. His job occasionally involved dealing with people, but he spent most of the time working alone in an immaculate and spacious office. There was an entrance that was solely used by Mr. Lee. He was the same level, but above others. Q4 workers at Hyunsoo's office wished to be like him. When Hyunsoo was busy considering the lunch menu, others were wondering what Mr. Lee's life was like.

"Good afternoon." Mr. Lee emphasized the afternoon. Hyunsoo tidied his look before entering the room, but couldn't hide the holes on the sleeve. Mr. Lee's eyes spotted them. "I reviewed your level record." Hyunsoo was physically there, but his conscious wasn't. Standing in front of the boss was because of a habit, following the computer's order. His conscious wasn't active.

"You are relegated to Q5.", "Did you get my message?" Hyunsoo asked. "Yes, two of your actions this morning affected your relegation. First, you were late. Second, you disgusted the people around you.", "Is it wrong to be upset when your loved one is taken away from you?"

Mr. Lee's eyes resembled the others from earlier this morning. He wasn't sure if it was because he used the word 'love' or the fact that he asked questions. Hyunsoo clearly felt there was a distinction between him and the others. "I wish I could help you. But rules must be kept. You should've handled your personal feelings better." Hyunsoo jumped over Mr. Lee's desk and punched him. He became Q6 like that.

Hyunsoo's credit of 120 flashed on the driver's seat. It

wasn't even enough for a meal. Being a taxi driver wasn't a bad job at all, he thought. Going by taxi was the only transportation in Shubble except people above Q3; they owned their vehicles. It wasn't going to be easy to become Q4 again. Earning credit wasn't reliable and there was more contact with people. But it didn't matter for Hyunsoo anymore. It was an emptiness that mattered to him. What happened during the day didn't feel like reality.

Hyunsoo sat in his new used car and watched the city illuminating. It was the same city he lived in, but it didn't feel the same. He felt miserable, but somehow also felt freedom. He knew one thing for sure, the city was beautiful.

An alarm went off. It was the first passenger.

2 Club Rodeo

Hyunsoo arrived to pick up the passengr. It was a big, round-shaped luxurious building. Of course, the taxi drove itself. There was subtle light on the surface of the building. He had a hard time finding a parking area. He cruised around for a while. Hyunsoo wondered the reason why they needed taxis. They must have their private hovercar. Finally, when he found where to park, a woman's long slender legs and smooth curvy hips were revealed.

Hyunsoo opened the passenger door. He was getting uncomfortable thinking about what would be appropriate for his first customer. There was something about her making him nervous. He breathed heavily. It made his voice unnatural. "Welcome!" Silence followed. She typed her destination instead of answering. "This is..." He turned around, but she still didn't say a word. And she didn't look like she would. *27 District H, Club Rodeo*

District H was where hybrids lived. They had no credit or level. He'd never been to District H. When Q6 couldn't maintain the level, they donated themselves to the hybrid experiments mixing human and animal. Once they experienced it, they were neither human nor animal. Hybrids were abandoned. They settled outside of Shubble and weren't allowed to come back to the city. Whatever happened in District H had nothing to do with Shubble. Hyunsoo realized how close he was to become a hybrid. Surprisingly, it didn't sound too bad. It almost sounded fun.

The woman immediately transferred 1,000 credits. She could see his credit from the passenger seat. She must have thought that he didn't want to go to District H. He kept forgetting he was the driver. The engine started with a shudder. The woman held on to the strap. "I am sorry, she's a bit old. No, I don't mean you." Hyunsoo had never felt stupid before. The woman was waiting with grace.

There were two tunnels on the edge of Shubble. One was for departing and the other was for returning to the city. It was so easy going to District H. Coming back, however, was a different story. All vehicles and citizens had to be searched thoroughly. They had to cross the border on foot. They sent out a blood sample under a stun gun's threat. While citizens were being checked, their vehicle was examined by spider robots. The robots scanned and analyzed every single object inside it. All the contents were already recorded as a computer had kept track of when who purchased what. It was illegal to take anything out of District H. The robots treated and searched everyone as if they were already guilty. Even if they had nothing to hide, they got nervous. Stun guns increased tension.

Someone screamed. The man must have gotten shot by a stun gun. He was vomiting and shaking his body so hard that he kept slamming his head, arms, and legs on the floor. A spider robot found a little bottle in his car. The robot held the bottle high to show off. The bottle came up on little screens next to people lined up waiting to be examined. However, Hyunsoo and the woman flew through the long, mundane tunnel.

At the end of the tunnel, it was another world compared to Shubble. Many of the people were citizens. But nobody was neat and tidy. There was a man who put his arm around a female hybrid full of hair, a man who was battling with a man hybridized with a cat, a hybrid couple mating on the street, and so on. Everyone looked so natural and nobody seemed to care, which felt different from people in the city who didn't care what happened to Hyunsoo this morning. There weren't any rules to follow and they didn't seem to care. Hyunsoo had never felt this relaxed before.

Club Rodeo was crawling with hybrids. Male hybrids were lined up at the entrance to get in. Most of them had quite threatening looks. Hyunsoo took a peek at the passenger seat. She sent a message from the back seat. *Wait for me. You will get another 1,000 credits on the way back.* She was waiting for him to open the door. He should have known. But he looked at the club again and was starting to getting worried. *Do you need an escort?* Hyunsoo typed the question. At that moment a smile crossed her face and etched in his mind. She opened the door herself.

As soon as she got off she drew all the attention of the male hybrids outside of the club. She walked slowly, which emphasized her curvy figure. When she approached, they stepped back and made a way for her. Soon, she disappeared into Club Rodeo.

1,120. He looked at his credit. It would last him a few days. Bitie wasn't at home anymore, so he could wait and earn 1,000 more credits. Hyunsoo thought about what he was going to do with it. It would be enough to buy another hybrid pet. But he wasn't going to. He thought of Bitie being sick, thrashing his sleeve desperately. He could practice manually driving. He thought about few more things and fell asleep.

He wasn't sure how long he'd been asleep. It'd been a long day. He had aches all over. He sat up and looked at his pale reflection in the mirror. He decided to find her and charge her credit for waiting. He thought he deserved it.

Club Rodeo
The Wildest of the Wildest

He laughed at the poster and walked into the club. He thought she had a hell of a unique taste. The level of taste didn't always reflect the level of social status.

There were many rooms down the long and narrow hallway. Hyunsoo was looking inside one of the rooms when a hybrid wearing a uniform walked out. It was an interesting scene: a half-naked female hybrid and two other legs between her thighs. As he walked down the hallway, he was getting close to a loud sound. At the end of it, there was a huge hall with a center stage. There were wasted citizens of Shubble and hybrids. Alcohol and drugs were scattered on the tables. It was odd to look at uptight normal Shubble citizens getting along with hybrids who had substantially different looks. He was thinking if he would ever come back here, or if he would settle down in District H. Maybe he could do a lap dance in a secret room like the one he saw earlier. If he was lucky, he might meet a big tipper.

When a man with a cowboy costume jumped onto the stage and grabbed the microphone, the loud music died down. His voice filled the hall. "Welcome to the wildest of the wildest games in District H." The crowd roared. He shouted, "Who wants to be a cowboy?" The crowd roared louder. The man bent over to listen to one of them. The man was overly excited about the game. It was Mr. Lee. He gave the cowboy a big nod. He looked a mess. Hyunsoo felt a bit guilty about bruising his eye. The cowboy was back to the microphone. "Wanna know how you can be a cowboy?" Mr. Lee and the crowd cheered. "Don't you worry boy, Toby will help you." The light shined on a shy bartender named Toby, who hybridized with an elephant. He greeted the crowd with a wave. The light ran over the center stage to illuminate the egotistic cowboy once again. Thanks to the light, Hyunsoo found the person who he was looking for. She was with a wolf. It was obvious this guy fell for her. The wolf was trying to impress her by explaining what was happening on the stage, but she looked bored. Hyunsoo stood in front of them.

"What do you want?" The wolf stood up aggressively as if he was protecting her. But the passenger greeted Hyunsoo with a big friendly smile. "Hey, have a seat.", "I think you owe me time and credit." Hyunsoo heard the anger in his own voice. She smiled again. Her smirk was annoying this time. The level wasn't an issue for him anymore. He could get into trouble one more time and apply to become a hybrid. Once he broke the rules, there was no limit on what he could do. "Only if you join us," she responded. "Come on, sit down. Please, I am buying you a drink." It was a harmless intention. Hyunsoo suddenly felt guilty about being angry.

When Hyunsoo sat next to her, she whistled. She signaled to Toby for two drinks and he signaled back. A waiter came with two greenish drinks. "These are cool. No matter how much you drink, these don't give you hang over." She leaned over to Hyunsoo so he could hear her well. She treated him like a friend. "For the past and present," she said. "And the future," Hyunsoo added. He really didn't know what was going to happen in his life. And he was looking forward to it. They toasted. She gulped. So did Hyunsoo. He immediately coughed violently. He felt fire going down his stomach. It quickly spread into his body and brain. He even had tears in his eyes. It made her laugh. Again, it was harmless. The wolf didn't like what was going on at his table. "This is Robbie, and this is...", "Hyunsoo." She introduced the two males to each other. The werewolf, Robbie, asked for a handshake and grabbed Hyunsoo's hand as hard as he could. "And I'm Huiwon." She gently held their hands and separated them.

Loud music announced the Rodeo was about to begin. As the center stage spun, the cowboy jumped off from it. As the stage split, a guy with a tie slowly emerged from underneath. He was sitting down on something and it was hard to see because of the metal fence. The new stage positioned in the center "Five, four..." The cowboy stood among the crowd and encouraged them to shout with him. Everyone in the hall started to count down with him. Huiwon shouted too. "Three, two, one." Finally, "Zero!" The fence folded down, revealing the raging bull. The man on top held onto the small handle on its back. The more the bull ran with anger, the more the crowd got excited. The bull didn't miss the opportunity when the man's hands slipped from the handle. The bull tossed the man into the crowd. They made sounds of pity then soon moved on to another rodeo on stage.

"Come with me." A hybrid came and talked to Hyunsoo. "I signed you up," Huiwon said. "Why did you do that?" Hyunsoo wanted to hear more, but he was following the hybrid and she waved her hand kindly. "On my way. Hi, I'm Alan. The next cowboy..." Alan walked and talked to someone in his earphone and to Hyunsoo all at the same time. "Pick one." The huge space underneath the center stage was full of bulls. They all were locked in individual cages and looked angry. Hyunsoo chose the young one with a little white spot on its nose. "This one, please." Alan stopped talking into his earphone. He looked at Hyunsoo and the bull. "Excellent."

Alan laughed and put an old harness on him. "Is this safe?" Alan laughed again. The harness made a clicking noise. After a few more clicks, Hyunsoo was lifted and had to stay in the air for a while. He could hear the banging sound of the raging bull and the excited crowd above his head. A run-down robot took the cage out under his legs. His bull was small. He was satisfied with his choice, watching over the small back of the bull.

When the cage set to the right position, he was lowered onto the bull. There was space to put in his legs next to the cage. When Hyunsoo's legs were in the right place, Alan released the harness quickly. Hyunsoo pushed up with the bull. The stage was opening up. The bull moved around a bit. Hyunsoo felt its strength. Something must be wrong. It was young and small, and supposed to be weak. He looked down Alan. He was smiling. "Have fun." He wanted to take back his choice but it was too late. He was already on stage. As the cage folded, the little bull started to move. He held on the handle tight.

The young bull bucked. It wasn't too bad riding it. When he felt like it was almost like dancing, it got faster. The bull soon reached a speed he couldn't keep up with. But it knew exactly what it was doing. The bull danced faster and faster. It controlled the game. When Hyunsoo's body was totally at its mercy, the bull stopped. Hyunsoo flew and the crowd's eyes followed him till he hit the wall and slide down onto the floor. The bull was relaxing on the stage. Again, the crowd made sounds of pity, then quickly turned back their focus on the next game. Only one person was interested in how he was. "Are you okay?" It was her, Huiwon. She helped him stand up with a smile. "Let's get back."

"Wait." Robbie grabbed her arm. It was interesting the

way they acted with each other. It couldn't be natural to have physical contact unless... they were in a relationship. It intrigued Hyunsoo's curiosity. There was no doubt that she was attractive, but it wasn't common for such a high-level woman to be with a hybrid. What was her story?

"Do you have a problem with that?" Hyunsoo said. He didn't know where that came from. Maybe it was the drink talking. It wasn't clear who picked the fight first. Hyunsoo didn't stop punching and wouldn't give him a chance to hit back. It was District H. Nobody cared what he did here. He wasn't afraid of losing credit or being a hybrid. Nothing to fear!

It didn't take that long to realize there was still something to be afraid of. It wasn't very wise of him to beat up a hybrid where hybrids lived. All hybrids in the hall surrounded him. "You aren't going back." Robbie stood up and wiped the blood from his lips.

"Be polite, you freak." It was Mr. Lee stepping in. One of the hybrids punched Mr.Lee on the face and it soon turned into an all out brawl of citizens against hybrids.

Huiwon held Hyunsoo's hand and started running. Hyunsoo set his car to full speed. The mode accidently went to manual and it refused to change back to automatic. "Damn!"

Prrrrrr, prrrrrr... He couldn't even start the engine. His new old car shook violently. Hybrids from the club were getting closer. "Can't you drive?" Huiwon's voice was calm. She broke the glass between the driver and passenger seat with her heel. She came over and sat down between his legs. When she turned on the ignition, the car lifted itself smoothly and she drove away. It was a relief. Well, for a moment. "They're following us!" Hyunsoo made a fuss. Huiwon checked their location on the GPS, took a sharp turn, and shook them off. She drove fast, but gently. While the hybrid chased them, they crashed into buildings and other vehicles.

Hyunsoo and Huiwon were getting close to the exit. There was only a tunnel between them and Shubble. The only problem was that there was a long line of cars ahead of them waiting to get through. The hybrids' cars surrounded them. "Do something!" Hyunsoo shouted, but Huiwon didn't seem to care. She sped up and drove through the tunnel above all the other vehicles. It set the alarm off. The roof tore off from his car. "Are you crazy?!"

When they entered Shubble, Huiwon stopped when the armed robots besieged them. They raised their arms to show they had no intention to revolt. The robots sent them home. Hyunsoo could tell the simple procedure was all because of Huiwon. She drove back home. Her home. She glided and parked gently. She hopped off from the convertible.

Hyunsoo was wondering if it was all over. He wondered if he could go back. He was going to ask for credit, but she drove. And damaged the car. Badly. He was going to talk about it. "Come in. It's late and you can't even drive," she said.

She walked down the corridor which was decorated in gold and reddish pattern. Subtle light made it more luxurious. Hyunsoo followed her. He also followed the lines of her body. The curves she had and her elegant movements were intoxicating. She twisted the door handle. He put his arm around her waist. She closed the door. And her red dress slipped down. Their bodies intertwined. They pushed each other toward the bed, each trying to take the lead. They tumbled over before they reached the bed.

Huiwon was on top of Hyunsoo. She smiled with satisfaction. He smiled too until he noticed something behind her back. She stabbed him between his eyes with a syringe. He lost consciousness, feeling a sharp pain.

3 Labyrinth

Hyunsoo was standing in a dark, narrow aisle. But, where was he and why was he there? He couldn't figure out where it began or ended. As he walked, it moved. As he stopped, it stopped. It changed its path along with his steps. He touched the wall. It was wet and sticky. The maze was alive. Hyunsoo could feel that it was watching him. He stood still. He waited and watched until the maze stopped. When it stopped, he stared and stared until it settled down and relaxed. Then he made a run for it. The maze started to move and tried to catch him. But he ran faster and faster, further and further. When he reached an open space, he stopped running. He breathed heavily.

"I'm going to get him!" "Hyunsoo, no. Come back!" The boys sounded familiar. They are young Hyunsoo and his brother, Phin. The maze takes him to his childhood when he is eight years old. He watches the two boys. He sees what young Hyunsoo sees, he feels what young Hyunsoo feels. He is there, but the two boys don't seem to notice. Hyunsoo heads to a park.

Phin is 10 years older than him, and bigger and stronger. Phin acts like Father, trying to fill the void since Father is always busy. But Phin often goes too far. Watching his childhood reminds him of how he used to feel about his brother. It is annoying.

Hyunsoo is heading to an old and rundown park. It was abandoned a long time ago. Nobody visits or takes care of it anymore. It almost looks like a forest. It is foggy and damp, but Hyunsoo enjoys the rare opportunity to explore a new place. He goes deeper and deeper. He finds a fountain. Hyunsoo carefully walks by a little bird taking a bath. He doesn't think the water is safe to drink. Right there, he finds footprints! He put his feet in them. They're huge. He follows them. It must be very close to what he is searching for, a serial killer. He shivers with excitement.

It's disappointing what's waiting for him at the end of

them. Phin is looking down at him. Phin has the familiar look, which Phin gives him whenever he breaks the rules. His face is accusatory. "There is no serial killer," Phin says. "What do you know?" Hyunsoo asks. Phin sighs deeply and puts a surgical mask on Hyunsoo's face. "You might catch a cold. We'll look around then go home." Hyunsoo kind of likes his concern and dislikes it at the same time. As annoying as Phin is, he is the only person Hyunsoo can count on. Phin walks ahead of Hyunsoo and makes it easier for Hyunsoo. But when Hyunsoo steps in a puddle of mud, Phin says, "Look what you've done." It pisses Hyunsoo off for a while.

The two boys walk for an hour and find nothing. Hyunsoo is getting tired. And he knows Phin has food and drink in his bag. All they have found is a rusty trail sign with a vague map of the park. "We've looked through most of it, and I'm getting tired. Let's get back.", "I'll take your bag. You can go." Phin knows what Hyunsoo is thinking. It's obvious that Hyunsoo won't go back for another few hours. Phin can't let that happen. Phin looks at his watch to figure out how behind schedule he is. He is supposed to finish homework by now, but he can't leave his younger brother alone. Hyunsoo is Phin's responsibility, since parents are busy. According to the map, there is a shelter not too far away. Phin suggests stopping at the shelter.

The shelter is cold and damp. A couple of dusty desks and chairs are all over the place. Phin lays down a picnic mat and takes out water, fruit, a chocolate bar, and vitamins, which Hyunsoo takes every day. Phin keeps looking at his watch. Hyunsoo grabs a chocolate bar and explores the shelter. Phin doesn't like what Hyunsoo is doing. All Phin thinks about is going back home. Phin devours all the food, frustrated by his unpredictable brother. Big brother hears Hyunsoo vomiting.

Hyunsoo's body is reacting to the disgusting smell. The room Hyunsoo is in is full of half-eaten dead animals. Hyunsoo is vomiting, but excited. He is hoping to find a skull to take to school. He covers his nose with his sleeve. "There's nothing to be afraid of. They're all dead." He talks to himself and starts to dig into the pile.

"I am disappointed in both of you." It's Mom. She is worried about how Phin resembles Father: hardworking, polite, punctual, but uptight. She has been hoping he'd develop a brotherhood by looking after his younger brother, but instead he sees it only as a responsibility.

Mom drags the two of them out of the shelter. She looks angry, but oddly enough the two boys start laughing when they see each other. "What are you laughing at?" Mom starts laughing, too. It has been a while to have a family outing since Father has gotten busy. It feels like a family picnic to them. "There must be a human skeleton in that pile. Can I look one more time? Please, Mom?" Hyunsoo asks. "There isn't," she replied. "Mom, they said on TV that the serial killer was hiding here, you heard that, too!", "Hyunsoo, don't believe everything you hear."

Mom stops. A giantic man is standing in front of them. Mom pulls her boys to her side. The man walks toward them. The way he walks is threatening. His huge shoes are covered in mud. Whenever he takes a step, Hyunsoo feels like a ground shake. The man looks at each one of them. "I know these faces." The man speaks with hatred. Mom hides two boys behind her. "Let the children go." Mom sounds as threatening as the man. He pulls back slightly. "Phin, go, take your brother with you."

Phin grabs Hyunsoo's hand tightly. When they walk past the man, Phin is terrified. The man walks closer to Mom. Hyunsoo sees the man's face and looks back at Mom. Hyunsoo doesn't understand what they are doing and what is going to happen. "Mom!" Hyunsoo is still tied up to Phin's arm. "Let go of me." The man turns around, holding Mom and faces the two boys. He takes out a knife and stabs Mom in the neck and cuts down her throat. Mom lets out a laborious cry. *RUN*

Phin covers Hyunsoo's eyes with his hand. Hyunsoo listens to the sound of Mom's life fading, and giggles with satisfaction.

4 Agony

Hyunsoo woke up screaming. He wondered where he was. It was a bedroom. Huiwon lit a cigarette. She was naked. She crossed her legs and looked at him. She must be thinking that he was cute. He felt something was dangling on his forehead. It was the syringe. It hurt taking it out. "Did you find anything interesting in your memory? It was especially made for you." She exhaled the smoke. "So, what did you see at the end of the maze?" She smiled. She must have planned all this and enjoyed watching it. "It is called a Sling. It helps you to find the memory you've lost.", "Who are you?" Hyunsoo asked.

Someone walked into the room. It was Phin. Hyunsoo jumped up and pushed him against the wall. "It's all your fault!" Phin was surprised but calm. "You need to put some clothes on." Hyunsoo realized he was still naked. He thought of last night: the red silk dress, her soft skin and the smell of it, and the Sling. "I believe you two have met already," Phin said. "This is my wife." Phin was still calm and didn't seem to care to see his wife and brother naked together.

He continued the conversation. "I don't know what you are talking about," Phin said. "We could've saved Mother!" Hyunsoo said. Phin saw Hyunsoo's eyes, full of anger thinking of the day. Could they have? Phin didn't think they could. They were too young. The day was lucid to Hyunsoo as if it happened yesterday, but it was 20 years ago. It was in the past for Phin. He discovered how Hyunsoo conjured up those thoughts. When Phin's eyes saw the Sling and Huiwon smiling, he was sure what it was about.

"You should remember why we were there. The man is the first generation of hybrid. The one that Dad made. You could sneak out that day because he escaped and our parents got distracted. If you were well behaved, Mom wouldn't have been there." It was true. Mom wouldn't have had to search for them if Hyunsoo stayed at home.

"It was more than an 8-year-old boy could handle, so Dad

and I decided to erase it from your memory. It was better that way for everyone. Furthermore, I am in the process of fixing the defects of the first generation. I experiment every aspect of all possibilities."

Hyunsoo struggled to catch up on what happened and what was happening. He felt guilt and regret. "Where is the man?", "He was never found." Huiwon put her arm around Hyunsoo and stroked him. She smiled at Phin. "Why didn't you find him?" Hyunsoo yelled. "What made you think Dad and I didn't?" Phin answered. "Cause you haven't." Hyunsoo left the room slamming the door.

The brothers were still annoyed by each other even after 20 years. Phin frowned. Huiwon didn't miss it. She knew exactly what it meant. He lost his temper. She put music on and danced to it. It was a celebration of a small victory. Phin grabbed her wrist "This doesn't change anything." His emotionless voice took her smile away. She would do anything to hurt him. But the more she tried, the more she hurt herself. She was left alone in the room. Only music filled the air.

4 Agony

As Hyunsoo walked to his car, he knew it wasn't Phin's fault. He felt enraged. He couldn't remember how to start the piece of junk. He screamed and shook the handlebar releasing his anger. The handlebar broke off. He got out and kicked his car. It made a sharp noise dragging itself on the floor. He didn't stop kicking it until it fell off the building. It wasn't enough. Hyunsoo threw the handlebar at it. The fact that he couldn't do anything made him explode.

5 Vector, Inc.

Phin's feet moved quickly. A massive X-shaped structure supported the inside of the Vector, Inc. building. Thousands of laps wrapped around the structure. He got on the elevator passing through the X, thinking about how he would arrange his work for the day efficiently. He checked what the time was. He was late. Nine hundred and seventy-three computers and one hundred and eighty-one robots were helping him. He still didn't have time for an unexpected event, such as his younger brother turned up, who hadn't seen for two decades.

Phin started from Section A. There was a long line of participants for hybrid experiments. There was strong, thin glass between him and them. He reviewed files for each one of them. All the information about them was recorded in the files, from general information to their genetic background.

Computers analyzed and made patterns of their behavior. Then, it suggested the three most practical experiments they can be used for. Phin's job was to make the decision of which experiment they would be sent to. There were even more participants on the conveyer belt waiting for him. Of course, they didn't know there was a delay.

His schedule was set to the minute and he usually spent about two minutes going over a file. He decided to spend less than a minute reviewing this time. He scanned the files as quickly as he could and then headed to Section M, where samples for hybridization were stored.

One of the participants appeared right in front of him and banged the glass. It wasn't unusual to see some participants go mad because they couldn't handle the pressure. This time it was a middle aged woman. Her hands were rough and her face was covered with tears and fright. Phin thought her skin looked like leather of a wild animal.

HELP! Her silent scream reminded him of his Mother. He thought of that day for a split second. Then he called for a stun gun as usual. She was out of her line. The woman lost consciousness. Machines moved her body onto another conveyer belt. Her body bounced a few times and was carried by a different conveyer belt. The computer moved her file away. She would be back the line the next day with the other participants.

He assisted father since he was young when his father stayed all day and night in his lab to get the first fund. When father's partner, Dr. Chang, disappeared to District H, he took over Dr. Chang's position. The experiment was not only the father's expectation but also the only way to communicate with father. He dedicated his life to father's experiment. There's only one thing he designed himself, however, which wasn't related to any of father's work.

***

As soon as Huiwon woke up she thought of what she was going to do that day. Robbie woke up. It was hard not to when they were sleeping on a single bed. It was also hard not to notice how she felt. He was going to ask if she was okay, but he didn't. They were Q6 and spent all their credit last night. There was only one place they could go.

They left early. A lot of participants had arrived already. They joined the line. All they needed was a drop of blood to apply for the experiment. Huiwon thought it was unusually painful for a normal credit check. Robbie exaggerated the pain. Maybe it was different for real. They could see the computer analyzing their information based on their blood. The computer identified each participant's information and history. It also made a list of diseases each participant was immune and subject to. It sometimes blinked to search for the right experiment and match ongoing and future experiments.

Huiwon saw a pale looking guy behind the glass. He watched what the computer did and how it occasionally moved the files around. She watched the computer analyzing her file. It listed the name of experiments on a few screens and waited for a decision to be made. She saw a man behind the glass and he saw her, too.

The signs led her to a small room. There was a desk, two chairs, and a light. She sat and waited for the next sign. The room was almost too clean to allow any living creature to survive. Maybe the experiment began already. And it wasn't surprising. She believed that there must be a reason why she was designated to a different conveyer belt from the others. And it must be related to the man she saw. The man entered and sat in front of her. He wrote something on his tablet and showed it to her. *Marry me.*

***

Huiwon had quick reflexes and protective instincts according to her file. She was impulsive but also in control in any circumstances. It was difficult to believe that she went down to Q6. She should be at least Q4 or above. "What did she spend all her credit on?" Phin wondered.

Phin searched her credit record. The majority of it was spent at District H. He wanted to know what she did in District H. But there was no way to find out. He was never so curious about a participant before. He was eager to learn more about her. He searched for her address. Another participant's name, Robbie, came up. His relatively good appearance and an assault laden record told him many things. He had seen enough participants like Robbie. Even Robbie's genetic information didn't deserve his attention. He was back to Huiwon's file.

While he repeatedly studied her, Phin came up with a different set of experiments. He injected Q2 and a nanorobot in Huiwon's blood. The robot flew inside her body and identified every single detail and adjustment. The robot also reported the time she woke up, where she went, what she ate, and what she did. It sometimes appeared under her skin, Phin never thought it would affect her life. Maybe it was because it didn't affect his.

4:25 A.M. Huiwon woke up feeling a cold metal object moving on her forehead. The bed wasn't small. It was the next thing she felt. As she turned her body over, she could see the finely decorated spacious room. She felt the embroidered duvet. It was all simple exchanges from one to another. She didn't miss Robbie, either. She certainly felt relieved that she didn't have to worry about her credit anymore. She had a chance to avoid being hybrid and took it. Exploring Vector,

Inc. took a long time. She saw all the different kinds of experiments Phin was conducting. By the time she was tired of exploring, she noticed what the nano-robots were doing.

"How was your day?" She asked. She knew exactly what his day was like. All planned, nothing unexpected, everything considered important, but boring. She was just asking to start a conversation. It was the first time to speak that day. Phin didn't seem to care. He acted like she wasn't there standing next to him. He finally noticed her presence when he saw the robot's red light under her skin.

Phin turned her over and went inside of her. She tried to get away from him but it was a useless effort when he grabbed and pulled her hair. She wanted to scream, but her voice failed to emerge. Pain dominated her body and soul until he finished with his rhythm. She understood what marriage meant to Phin.

4:25 A.M. Huiwon was thinking of last night. It was going to be repeated. She had to escape. To escape, she had to be calm. The first thing she had to do was to get rid of the robot. It was passing on her forehead. She concentrated on its movement. *Gotcha!*

It disappeared as if it wasn't there. She focused again. While searching for it, she felt the most wretched feeling toward it that she never felt before. The robot showed up on her collarbone, it sent her emotional status to Phin. It stayed there waiting for her to catch it. As soon as she pinched it, it slides back in and hid. The robot teased her. She wanted to tear herself off.

She remained calm and steady. She went to the bathroom as if she had given up. She washed her face, feeling the robot glide in her arm. She quickly tied her upper arm tight. As the blood pumped faster the robot was carried in. She cut her arm open and squeezed. The robot finally was found as the blood flowed.

Huiwon wrapped her arm with a towel. She didn't see anyone or a thing on her way to the parking lot. She hopped on a hovercar and typed District H as her destination. She tied her arm tighter. At that moment, she felt a metal object in her eye. Another robot stretched up her tear duct. It unfolded its legs, crawled over her head, and poked her with a long needle.

When she woke up, she was in a bedroom. The red light from the robot was blinking. *You are in a different set of experiments from other participants. The experiment can't be done without you.* It was what Phin wrote to her on a computer message. Phin looked sorry when he wrote it. He was on top of her this time. He was giving unfortunate participants a break. She had no strength to resist.

Thanks to his scientific brutality, soon she got pregnant. The robot's work had doubled. It sent off her status as well as the baby. The baby grew with her affection and hatred. Phin couldn't hide the excitement monitoring the baby each day. He was excited because of his new experiments he could do with it. When he finished setting up a new lab, Huiwon showed up. "You didn't want to raise it, did you?" Phin couldn't tell if she intended to. She didn't answer. "Well, if you did, the next one can be yours." She stared and walked away.

The next morning, Phin made Huiwon come to the new lab. He gave her a shot in the arm. "You are going to give birth today.", "Let me do it myself." She ran into the delivery room and locked herself in. She picked a blade and stood where Phin could see her properly. She sliced open her belly and removed the baby. Phin tried to open the door. She rolled the umbilical cord around her own baby's neck. Her baby and Phin were screaming. She felt guilt and pleasure simultaneously. Phin managed to open the door and attempted to save the baby. She watched it lying and bleeding on the floor. She knew the baby wouldn't survive as she closed her eyes. She also knew she was going to feel guilty for rest of her life and not satisfaction.

6 District H

Hyunsoo was in a taxi. He gave all his credit to the unhappy driver who wasn't keen on going to District H. Hyunsoo was in pain sitting behind the driver's seat. His memory was almost too clear to contain. It felt like pieces of memory cut his brain open. Instead of trying to forget, he scanned them thoroughly and faced all the details.

The shelter, the way it smells of dead animals.

The voices, the way Mom and Phin laugh.

The man's eyes, the way he looks at her.

The man's body, the way he holds her.

The man's hand, the way he handles the knife.

The sounds, the way Mom screams; *RUN!* the way the man chuckles.

The taxi sped away as soon as Hyunsoo got off. He was alone on a busy street. Some people were tangled up in each other. He didn't know where to begin. There must be someone who knew the man. He wanted to believe so. "I am looking for the first generation hybrid, he is about this tall..." People passed by. He felt so stupid. He was describing a man from 20 years ago. He walked to Club Rodeo knowing it was a bad idea.

It was indeed. When he stepped into the hall, the rodeo and the music stopped. All hybrid turned around and looked at him with hostility. One of them stood in his way. Hyunsoo wanted to address his incensed eyes. "I am not here to fight.", "We ain't care why you are here. The fact that you are here is what we care about." He was being beaten on before he realized it. "I'm looking for the first generation of hybrid." There might be someone who knew the man he was searching for. He kept shouting feeling several types of feet and their strength, and even a bite here and there.

"Please, stop, stop!" Someone begged. It was the shy bartender, Toby. Toby took Hyunsoo to storage full of alcohol. Toby sat him down and came back with the first aid kit. Hyunsoo had a chance to look at Toby closer. Toby's big round nose and triangle-shaped ears showed he was hybridized with an elephant. Toby had a wound circling his neck. He had a fungus growing on it. It seemed his wound had been cut off and closed up several times. The fungus kept growing back. It must be a side effect of hybridization. Hyunsoo's injury would eventually heal, but there wouldn't be a cure for what Toby had. Toby didn't have much time left. He may not have to be terminated like Bitie. However, eventually he was going to meet his demise. Most likely, all hybrids were enduring the same process, only matter of what type of symptoms.

Toby's hands told him that he was familiar with the situation. He didn't look like the kind that could deal with rough hybrids who enjoyed the rodeo. He was just too quiet and meek. He looked almost fragile. "First time here, right? It's been twelve years that I've worked here. I can tell who the newbies are. You've got to be more careful. People in District H are constantly looking for a fight. Most hybrids have mixed feelings toward citizens. They are visitors who bring big money, but they are also the reason why hybrids live in a separate area. If they see someone hurt a hybrid it's a good chance to get payback."

Hyunsoo felt shameful. Nobody considered a hybrid as a person in Shubble. And nobody cared when he was troubled in Shubble. He didn't know what to say about Toby's kindness, so he just said, "I am looking for the first generation of hybrid. He is about two meters tall, muscular, and has dark brown skin.", "Half of the hybrids can fit your description." Hyunsoo wasn't surprised. It was 20 years ago.

Toby added, "You are looking for the first generation, so you might want to talk to Dr. Chang. He moved here from Shubble when hybrids settled down. He provides all the booze in District H. I've heard he used to be the best scientist in Shubble. He has his own town now, we called it District L."

Toby called a cab and paid enough credit to get Hyunsoo home. Hyunsoo never saw anyone offer such hospitality. The series of events that happened in last two days were almost shocking. His life; waking up in a cell; going to work every morning; choosing the same lunch; coming back to his cell every night. At this point, it all felt so distant from reality.

He had a visitor in his cell. "Technically, we didn't sleep together." It was Huiwon. Hyunsoo didn't let himself go mad again. He decided to wait until she continued. "Don't be embarrassed. It was worth it. It was pretty entertaining to me at least," she paused. "Your memory too. I really enjoyed every single step of bringing it back to you." But she didn't look happy or pleased. Strangely, he felt pained when she said it. It was something he was familiar with. "What do you want?" Hyunsoo asked. "Comfort," Huiwon answered.

Hyunsoo put his hand on her skin. He felt her scars hidden behind her clothes and long hair. He didn't know where or how she got them. But he felt what she felt. He kissed every scar she had. They shared and comforted each other's pain.

7 District L

Everything was natural and smooth apart from Hyunsoo. Huiwon's car was spacious and stable. She drove it like it was part of her body. It was hard not to notice his discomfort. He squeezed himself in a little corner. She broke the silence. "I enjoy driving manually.", "I can see that." He answered like an angry child. "I used to drive a taxi like you. Driving became a hobby after marriage." She added to make him feel better.

District L was a giant farm. Hyunsoo and Huiwon flew above greenhouses. At the end of the greenhouses, they flew between cornfields where artificial light was shining on. The light changed its angle to shine on other parts of the field. After they flew through the unbearable heat they found a place to park.

There were two geometric towers. Each building was

spiral-shaped. But the light and heat didn't reach the buildings. The two towers were so dark and spooky. Hyunsoo heard something behind a parked freight car. Someone was wolfing down food from a can. His movements suggested he was a hybrid. He was too concentrated on food to realize that there was someone there.

"Excuse me," Hyunsoo said. The man was frightened and stood up quickly. He dropped his food on the ground. He was huge standing up. He took a glimpse of Hyunsoo and ran away. The way he ran was like a cross between human and giant mammal. Hyunsoo didn't mean to scare him off, but it happened.

Hyunsoo and Huiwon heard the sound of machines from one of the tower. When they went in, a drop of liquid fell off. They could still hear the sound of machines moving. It was still dark so they couldn't see much of what was there. A tired footstep was getting closer to them. Finally, a kid appeared from the darkness. They couldn't tell if the child was a boy or a girl. The child was so surprised to see them and couldn't close his or her mouth. The kid had a shiny bald head, two nostrils without a nose, and a pointy upper lip. And the kid's mouth was still left open. "Wake up!"

A middle-aged man came out from the darkness and hit the child very hard. Soon when the man found Hyunsoo and Huiwon, he pushed the kid away as if the kid was a shameful object to hide. "How can I help you?" He asked kindly. But there was an unpleasant feeling underneath his smile. "We are looking for Dr. Chang." Huiwon cut to the chase. Strangely the more he smiled, the more unpleasant it became. "I am Dr. Chang."

***

Dr. Chang showed Hyunsoo and Huiwon around his town, District L. It was even bigger than what they had already seen. "You won't survive without me. The liquor you imbibe in District H, it is all from here. When I say you, I mean District H as well as Shubble. You know why? All the food you eat in Shubble is from here too. And *I* am running District L."

Hyunsoo counted the number of greenhouses but shortly

gave up. It was not only confusing to listen to what Dr. Chang said but also there were too many of them. Huiwon didn't seem to care about the talk of Dr. Chang or the size of District L either. Dr. Chang took them to one of the greenhouses. He never stopped talking. It almost felt like noise to them.

Inside the greenhouse was full of the sweet, fresh scent of fruit. Each tall tree planted in a row was growing peaches on every branch. Children were dangling on trees, picking the peaches. "I grow peaches here. I have twenty of these just for peaches. Of course, I have the same number of greenhouses for apples, pears, and bananas." He took Hyunsoo and Huiwon to a corner of the greenhouse. A bunch of children was peeling peaches and chopping them into small pieces. They put five pieces each in a small box. When they sealed it with a heat presser, it turned into the processed lunch Hyunsoo used to eat at Subble.

All the children got on with their work as if Hyunsoo and Huiwon weren't even there. Most of them had burn marks on their hands and arms. It must have been from the presser. Some of them were missing a couple of fingers. "I am building seven more greenhouses to meet the consumption demands of Shubble. Hybrids are supposed to work faster, but as you can see they are all useless." Dr. Chang cut open one of the peach boxes and offered for a taste. Hyunsoo knew exactly what it tasted like and didn't feel like eating after seeing the marks children had. Hyunsoo asked, "Do you know the first generation of hybrid?" Dr. Chang carried on his tour. Hyunsoon thought he didn't hear.

Dr. Chang's tour took the whole day. Hyunsoo and Huiwon had heard enough. The lousy talker insisted on treating them to dinner. It was more for his benefit than theirs. He led them to a dining room. He lit some candles. "It's been a while since I had guests who I can talk to. I have prepared special food for special guests." Hyunsoo could see several children were busy preparing food in the kitchen. The kid they met earlier was there too. The kid didn't seem to know what he or she was supposed to do. The child was in the way of other children. Dr. Chang looked annoyed by it. The kid walked carefully with a bottle of alcohol and glasses. But with every step the child took, the alcohol overflowed. In a few more careful steps, the kid dropped the bottle. It fell off from the tray and shattered on the floor.

Dr. Chang grabbed the child. "Do you know how much this is? It is worth three times more than you.", "Hey, that's not how you treat a child." Hyunsoo stood and shouted. Dr. Chang settled and let the kid go. But the kid was shivering. Hyunsoo helped the child getting up. "Are you okay?" Hyunsoo asked but the kid ran away to the kitchen.

"I owe you an apology. She arrived only a few days ago, so she isn't used to the jobs here. She is useless now, but in a couple of years, she will be ready to be sold back to District H. She is a good investment.", "What do you mean by selling her?" Hyunsoo asked. "She is a half breed crossed between a hybrid and citizen, like most children here. Some have both hybrid parents.", "Where are their parents?" Hyunsoo asked. "How will I know? I buy them from brokers." Dr.Chang answered. Hyunsoo rephrased his question. "Do you mean their parents don't want to raise them?", "Why would anyone want to keep them? They are hybrids." Dr. Chang answered. The conversation ended abruptly.

Huiwon left the table, wandering around the room. The room was full of collections of alcohol. Some of them were in fancy bottles. Each had a label on them. She stood still in front of a glass column. She took a closer look at it. There was a child with a snake body and several legs. His eyes were vacant. "You have an eye for good alcohol. Let me do the honor of pouring you a glass straight from the barrel. Please, have a seat."

Dr. Chang put his arms around her and pushed her into the chair. She felt for sure he had been waiting for a chance to touch her. "The boy was notorious. Whenever he showed up, the whole district erupted in chaos due to his poison. The poison made him into a very fine drink." Dr. Chang twisted the tap of the column and filled three glasses. The boy and his legs waved gently with the flow of the liquid he was in. Hyunsoo didn't even want to touch the glass. The drink was such a pretty color, he thought. "This is the best brew I've ever made. Please, enjoy and accept my apology."

Dr. Chang stretched his arm and began to stroke Huiwon's hand. She flicked his hand away from her. She stared at Dr.

Chang and poured the drink on the floor. He gave her a sinister smile. Hyunsoo didn't like how District L operated. Dr. Chang was also bothered by his presence next to Huiwon. Dr. Chang frowned and shouted toward the kitchen. "Move faster, you idiots!"

Three girls appeared with a food trolley. They laid a big plate of meat in the center. One of them sat next to Dr. Chang, chopped the meat and served each person, one by one. Dr. Chang stroked the girl's thigh staring at Huiwon. She watched what he was doing and he was aware of it. Two other girls set the table with exotic food. However, Hyunsoo and Huiwon didn't want a bite any of it. Dr. Chang didn't seem to care and started shoveling the food into his mouth.

"Unlike others, I believe that hybrid children are worth raising. If I teach them right, they are worth as much as a fine drink." Dr. Chang spoke with his mouth full. His hands were also busy alternating between food and drink. "Most children born in District H are abandoned. It is such a struggle for hybrids to keep themselves alive, so raising children is simply too much for them. On top of that, their children are direct reflections of themselves, a disgusting existence. So, I pick them up, feed them, dress them, and provide places to sleep. If they are talented, I teach them and help them work at District H." Dr. Chang said.

Huiwon wondered how much of it was true. "That is very generous of you. What kind of education do you give them?", "Dancing and singing. It is the most useful technique to survive for hybrids. Especially for girls. I teach them other things, too. I can show you what it is if you'd like." He stroked Huiwon's arm with a finger. Hyunsoo jumped and stepped on his food. "You know why we came: The first hybrid.", "Why do you want to know something that happened such a long time ago?" Dr. Chang produced a wry smile. Hyunsoo grabbed his neck and held his fork against it. Dr. Chang realized that he couldn't avoid answering this time.

"It is the most powerful hybrid ever made. Also, it has a fatal flaw. All hybrids are result of failure experiment to correct it." Dr. Chang said. "What is the flaw?", "The ego confusion between humans and animals. It was hybridized between Taurus, the genetically modified super bull, and a man. He was healthy, physically and mentally. After the experiment, he had both characteristics of humans and animals. He was confused at every moment whenever he made small decisions. He achieved the strong body he wished for, but he couldn't control his mind. He was messed up badly."

"How do you know all this?" Huiwon asked. "Because it was *my* experiment!" Dr. Chang shouted. "Where is he now?" Hyunsoo's voice was aggressive. "It showed up once in a while in District H a few years ago. Who cares whether it's dead or not. It is only a fucked-up hybrid. Shit, now I lost my appetite." Dr. Chang walked away.

***

A small hand pulled Hyunsoo. "Follow me," it was the kid from dinner. "What is your name?" Hyunsoo gently asked. "Dizi," the kid answered. "Dizi, where are you taking us?" Dizi took Hyunsoo and Huiwon to the tower. There were spiral stairs inside the building. There were rooms along the side of the stairs, with five to six children in each room.

Huiwon tried to stay calm but she couldn't help being uncomfortable from all the attention of children. Some of them were curious, and others were cautious. One of them ran into Huiwon, tied arms around Huiwon's leg. Huiwon felt the child's temperature, breath, and strength of life. Huiwon couldn't move.

"Shall we stay here tonight?" Hyunsoo asked. He held Huiwon's hand and led her to one of the rooms. Children in the room fought to sleep next to Hyunsoo and Huiwon. Huiwon didn't want to see the chaos they'd caused. "Wait." She lay down in the middle of the room. Hyunsoo lay next to her. Children settled around them. Each of them had their share of Hyunsoo and Huiwon. Dizi snuck into the room and claimed the spot next to Hyunsoo. The floor was hard and uneven. But it wasn't too bad sharing the room with children.

8 Rodeo

Hyunsoo and Huiwon woke up early. The children got up early. They folded the covers and blankets they used overnight. Some of them hadn't even opened their eyes yet, but they knew what to do.

They lined up for breakfast and sat down on the ground. Breakfast was a bowl of porridge. By the time they were about to eat, it turned cold. Hyunsoo wasn't sure if it was edible. Huiwon didn't seem concerned. "Last night dinner looked great but you have to wonder what it was made of. We looked around the whole town and never saw any animals being raised. Where the meat came from was pretty questionable. But this is different. I don't think Dr. Chang would provide 'good food' to children. 'Good food' in his standards doesn't mean good food in my standards. So this is at least okay to eat." Hyunsoo tasted a bit of porridge. It wasn't as bad as it looked. He was relieved that it only tasted of vegetables.

Children had several bottles among them. Huiwon friendly approached them. They offered her one of the bottles. She figured out that it was alcohol they made. They put it in their porridge. She realized that their eyes were unfocused and their hands were shaky. Some had bright red faces and couldn't walk straight. They were drinking to get over their hangover from last night. Gradually, the children were becoming alcoholics.

It took them only a few minutes to finish their breakfast. They waited in line again to return their bowls. "Was it good?" Hyunsoo asked a boy who washed the dishes. He was older and taller than others. This teenager didn't say a word. He moved his hands from a dirty bowl to a clean bowl with precision.

All children who finished their breakfast disappeared to work. Hyunsoo looked at Huiwon. She was taking a walk. He thought they might have to go back to District H, starting all over again. He had to find the murderer no matter what.

He wondered how far she was prepared to go with him.

"Do you have something that tastes good?" It was the boy who cleaned up the dishes. "I'm Hakko." Hakko extended his hand for a handshake. Hakko's eyes on Hyunsoo were full of curiosity. "You have lived only in Shubble." Hakko said. "How do you know?" Hyunsoo wondered if it was that obvious. "I go to District H from time to time with Dr. Chang since I was little. Dr. Chang may act like he does everything, but there are things he can't do on his own. I take care of those tasks. I've learned who comes in and out, and what permanent resident in District H may look like." Hakko added.

"You were very efficient." Hakko didn't seem to understand what Hyunsoo meant. Hyunsoo pointed out the clean bowls Hakko finished. "Once Dr. Chang assigns a task, you are pretty much stuck with it forever. I've been washing the dishes ever since I came here." Hakko talked quietly but couldn't hide his excitement. Hakko was bright. Hyunsoo could understand why Dr. Chang chose Hakko as an assistant. There was something special about Hakko compared to other kids. "You are different." Hakko paused then continued. "Maybe that's because I don't drink." This time, Hyunsoo paused. "What made you not to drink?" Hakko started talking slowly. "I used to. I am not saying drinking is bad. I've seen some people who know when to stop." Hakko is surely thinking about the events that made him stop drinking. The boy asked quickly in anticipation, "Do you want to see how we make liquor?"

Hakko took Hyunsoo to the tower where children worked. "What you saw yesterday was packaging. Those boxes go to District H. What we do is really simple. We pick fruit, wash, dry, put them in alcohol, and finally ferment them. That's it."

"It doesn't look that simple." There was a fight between two groups of children. Anger and insanity radiated. It was something you wouldn't expect from children. Hakko jumped down and went into the middle of the fight. He split up the groups and gave different tasks to handle then came back up to Hyunsoo. "It happens all the time: The floor is uneven so dried fruits get wet easily. I keep asking Dr. Chang to get another table, but he doesn't really care."

Hakko took Hyunsoo to a room on the fifth floor. Only a few people must have access to it. When they entered it was too hard to breathe because of the heat. Hakko waived his arm and stirred up the heat. "I am steaming rice. When it is done, I'll spread it out here to dry. Then ferment it over there. And leave it for days to ferment." Hakko looked confident. It had a sour smell. The bubble was coming out from inside. It was alive. Hakko's eyes were filled with joy. "Come over here."

Hakko took Hyunsoo into a small room and stood next to a metal box proudly. "Do you want to try my *Makgeolli*?" Hakko gave Hyunsoo a cup of it. Hakko couldn't wait till Hyunsoo finished it. "How do you like it? Dr. Chang tastes it from time to time. He doesn't say much. So, it must be okay, I guess." It was more than okay. Hyunsoo gave him a thumb up to express his approval. It made Hakko's day. Hakko was enjoying having a guest. "If you don't drink, how do you make booze?" Hakko tapped his nose and smiled. "I taste some when I need to. The entire process of making it is fascinating: how individual ingredients turn into alcohol."

"Most people from Shubble haven't even heard of us. What brings you here?" Hakko asked. "I'm looking for a hybrid.", "What does he look like? Or is it she?" Hyunsoo sketched the face of the man as best he could. Just thinking of him brought back the memory and anger. A smile had disappeared from Hakko's face. "I have seen this man."

***

Hakko walked ahead of Hyunsoo and Huiwon. Hakko didn't say much. He was nervous. He said that Dr. Chang firmly restricted access to the building. "I haven't met the guy in person." Hakko turned around and talked to Hyunsoo. Hyunsoo put his hand on Hakko's shoulder. "Thank you." When Hakko unlocked the door, he rushed over to the computer which was at the opposite end. Hyunsoo followed him.

Huiwon took her time and walked around slowly. Half of the storage was more like a library. The dust showed that the books weren't used for a very long time. There was one side of a wall that was decorated with tiles. Each tile had an image on them. Huiwon took a closer look. They were portraits of the man they met in the parking lot. The man had the ugliest look she could imagine. He vaguely looked like a human. His body and face were covered with hair. The date was 11/30/2030. She followed the photographs. Each one was going back to the past and getting close to what he looked like originally. The closer to the past, the more the man looked like a human. She stood in front of the very first photograph of him.

Hyunsoo was looking at clips of Dr. Chang's experiment. The first generation of hybrid, he was the specimen of Dr. Chang's experiment. Dr.Chang photographed and filmed the entire process.

Profile
Name: Bo
Date: 03/01/2008
Specification: The first hybrid of Project X. Bo is hybridized with a man, who is a physically strong and healthy person, and a Taurus, which is a genetically modified super bull. Bo has strong characteristics of both.

8 Rodeo

Bo was harnessed to a machine, struggling with anger and pain. Bo was losing man's figure and mind. Dr. Chang's description followed; *Bo is confused about who he really is.* Dr. Kang, Hyunsoo's father and Dr. Chang came in and out with a drink and watched their experiment with merciless eyes. It didn't matter how drastically Bo morphed, Dr. Chang made a machine to fit him perfectly. When the clip was approaching the present time, Bo began to resemble the man Hyunsoo saw in the parking lot. The date stopped at 11/30/2030. Hyunsoo's heart was racing.

"You uncovered my biggest secret. He is the main energy source of District L. The machine I invented right there converts his anger into electricity. He is getting angrier these days." Dr. Chang wasn't at all offended. In fact, Dr. Chang was like the cat that swallowed the canary. He pushed Hakko away and carried on talking. "I am the best scientist in Shubble. Bo is one of a kind. He is the first hybrid and no other hybrid can compare to him. Because *I* made him." He was proud to divulge his secret.

"Well, Dr. Kang from Vector, Inc. helped me, but I pretty much did all the work. If you look at this picture, Bo's amygdaloid nucleus is three times bigger than a normal brain. The amygdaloid nucleus is the part of a brain that controls anger. He seemed to do well right after the hybridization. Dr. Kang and I reintroduced him to society and monitored. It was about a year after the experiment when he noticeably showed changes. He saw a guy beating up an old woman and couldn't hold his temper. He punched the guy to death. Bo scared everyone in site, it was clear Bo had been unnessarily violent. So, we brought him back to Vector, Inc. When I saw Bo again, he was completely different. We never expected Bo to evolve the way he did.

One night, I left early and maybe had left a couple of the doors open, but I didn't know he would escape. He was obedient, and never left his cage before. His escape wasn't my responsibility. But Dr. Kang accused me. Damn." Dr. Chang grunted. "Because he escaped and killed my mother." Hyunsoo said aggressively.

Dr. Chang looked into Hyunsoo's eyes and recognized a familiar look of an old friend. "I see, I see, you are the boy.

But, how?" His unpleasant smile appeared once again. "Of course, who can it be? I am the best scientist of all time! It was me who brought the memory back to you. By the way, I was the one who erased it when you were a little boy."

"Keep on laughing." Huiwon stabbed the Sling on Dr. Chang's forehead. "I didn't know about that. You've got to trust me," Huiwon added. Hyunsoo still had his doubts.

Bam! Something was banging on the door. Each time, it got stronger. Finally, the door slammed wide open. A dark heavy shadow casted upon the walls. Dr. Chang recognized the shape.

Hyunsoo saw the anger in Bo's eyes. "Hey, Bo. I know it's you. Let's talk." Hyunsoo approached him. Bo totally lost a man's figure. Instead, he became a powerful bull. Hyunsoo moved a step closer to Bo. Bo stared at him. The more Hyunsoo got closer, the angrier Bo grew.

Suddenly, a blank attacked Bo. He blinked. But he couldn't see anything and felt pain in between his eyes. Dr. Chang was standing in front of Bo. When Dr. Chang released his hand from Bo, the Sling was on Bo's forehead. Dr. Chang stepped backward and ran. Huiwon chased after him.

Bo watched Hyunsoo carefully. Hyunsoo was vaguely familiar, but at the same time, he wasn't. Bo focused on the memory and sense. In his brain, he was running through the memory maze. He ran and brought back all the memories of Shubble, District H, and District L. The experiment, Dr. Kang, Dr. Chang, a mother of two boys... the boy, Hyunsoo. When all the little pieces of his memory were back together in one piece, he experienced a sharp pain. Bo screamed and ran toward Hyunsoo. "Easy, control yourself." Bo missed and kept running into bookshelves, desks and everything in the storage while chasing after Hyunsoo. When Bo was close, Hyunsoo jumped. He landed on Bo's back and held on to his horn tightly.

Bo thrashed. The old building's walls were smashed. Bo and Hyunsoo crashed out of the storage. Hyunsoo was still on the back. Children surrounded them. Hyunsoo was gripping Bo's mane. Bo spun around to shake him off. Finally, Hyunsoo fell off Bo's back, and Bo didn't miss him this time. Bo rushed at him and speared him with his horn. Bo pushed

Hyunsoo into the wall and pierced Hyunsoo's stomach. Bo scratched the wall lifting his horn. Hyunsoo slid down. Bo looked at Hyunsoo to find fear and pain in his eyes.

"I'm sorry about what my father did to you." It drove Bo even madder. He threw Hyunsoo in the air. Children dashed to get Hyunsoo. But when Bo came back to finish him off, they stepped back. Hyunsoo stood up, leaped on Bo's back, and grabbed him by the horn. Hyunsoo held on tighter. Bo hurt himself trying to get Hyunsoo down. Both of them were covered in blood. And both got tired. "Have you had enough? Can we talk now?" Hyunsoo muttered and lost consciousness.

Bo took him to the forest where they were first met. It was foggy and chilly. Bo carried Hyunsoo like a friend. Hyunsoo got off, stroked Bo and looked into his eyes. There wasn't anger in them anymore. They walked side by side. They sat down on a hill where they could see the city. The city bustled as always. They must be working hard inside and out of the high-rise buildings, following computers' orders.

Hyunsoo couldn't bear the exhaustion and fell asleep

thinking Shubble was still a valuable place to save. When Hyunsoo woke up, Bo had vanished. He knew he would never find Bo again. And he didn't intend to do so. If they were supposed to meet, it would happen eventually. He had something else to do. He had to go back, back to Shubble.

9 The Virus

Hyunsoo looked out the window from Dr. Chang's office. The children were playing. They all looked different and moved differently. But still, they got on well.

"So, what happened to my Father?" Hyunsoo asked. Dr. Chang was tied to a chair making an unpleasant noise. When Huiwon took off the tape, he spat the bad taste from his mouth. "He may not be seen but he is everywhere. He is the system that drives Shubble."

Dr. Chang continued. "He became material with biological information yet he still has the characteristics of a life form. Dr. Kang went into the system as a virus. He spread out rapidly once he entered the system. Soon, he controlled all the computers in Shubble and changed the system into the one he dreamed of." Hyunsoo wondered, "Is he still alive?" "Oh, yes. He'll live forever." Hyunsoo wasn't sure if that was good or bad.

According to Dr. Chang, Phin took over the hybrid experiment from father. The experiment aimed to create a perfect hybrid between humans and animals. There were thousands of possible hypotheses to correct the flaw of the first generation, Bo. Phin was doing every single one of them at Vector, Inc. None were successful. Failed hybrids suffer from side effects.

"How many of experiments are there left?" Hyunsoo asked.

"As many as he has done to this day, maybe?" Huiwon said. "As far as I've seen, millions, even billions, of experiments are ongoing." She added. "There may be more. Every life has its own uncertainties, which is what makes each of us unique. The uncertainty causes unexpected results. The more he experiments, the more cases there are. In other words, the experiment will never end. It will produce more hybrids." Dr. Chang was excited. It was a promising foundation as the dictator of District L. "And more hybrids will make more children like them." Huiwon said.

"You want to stop the experiment, don't you?" Dr. Chang

spoke as if he read Hyunsoo's mind. "Because the children out there deserve a better life." Once Hyunsoo said that Huiwon looked at him with adoration for the first time. "How about vaccination?" She showed interest. "Wrong! It is only a precaution, not a cure. It's too late for that. Dr. Kang himself is the system now." Dr. Chang enjoyed showing off his knowledge.

"There must be a way." Hyunsoo murmured. "How about anti-virus? If Dad is a virus, an anti-virus might do the trick." Dr. Chang smiled like a child. "It is possible. There is a control tower which supplies power to Shubble and Vector, Inc. If we can insert the right protein into the system, it will detach the weak connection of DNA. It will create a malfunction in the system." Dr. Chang said with joy. "Will it affect the city?" Hyunsoo asked. "It can destroy the city, too." Hyunsoo had second thoughts. Even if so, it had to be done. Dr. Chang wore a bigger smile. Hyunsoo wasn't sure why Dr. Chang was so cheerful.

"It won't be easy. How will you get to the control tower?" Huiwon interrupted. "The security system is monitoring every exit. For example, my designated entrance records all movement, weight, and temperature. It even detects my step changes depending on what shoes I'm wearing. It is the way it works everywhere inside of Vector, Inc. If anything goes wrong, the labs shut down. The system protects the experiment first. Nobody can get in or out of the building without being monitored." Hyunsoo wondered, "How did I get in without the system knowing last time?", "You aren't thinking that nobody knew you were coming, are you?" Hyunsoo felt stupid.

"Would it be possible to divert the attention until everybody in the building can escape?", "That is an interesting idea. Making him numb can be possible. The system works, but it's not awake." Dr. Chang smiled again. It was a surprisingly genuine smile coming from pure curiosity and excitement. Now, Hyunsoo could understand the reason why his father decided to split up their partnership. Dr. Chang enjoyed the destruction itself. He wasn't interested in a better life for children and he would never be. But Hyunsoo still had to work with him as he was the best scientist apart from his

9 The Virus

father and brother. Dr. Chang was his only bet.

Dr. Chang never left his lab, working three days straight. He had a drink by his side at all times. His hands shook badly. His hands often struggled to hold the samples and sometimes broke them. When they did, he cursed at his own hands. After a few more drinks, he got back to work. When he was out of his lab, he had two little bottles, the yellow and the red.

"This Yellow is A-11, a local anesthetic which will buy us some time. The Red is S-09, an anti-virus which will be injected into the main computer in the control tower. Human DNA like you, me and that woman, is composed of nucleotides referred to as 'A, C, T, G.' Dr. Kang's DNA is different. When he was bonding with the system, proteins 'L, M, O, R' were made, which are completely new from any living creature. From there, like normal human DNA, they have been duplicated and formed the protein. That's how Dr. Kang knows everything in Shubble and controls all the situations immediately."

"So how do they work?" Huiwon interrupted. "You don't

even know the first thing about this." Dr. Chang was almost hysterical. He couldn't stand someone distracting his little presentation. He held S-09 higher up. "This red concoction may look unimpressive, but it contains special capsules in it. Enzymes in capsules will flow along Dr. Kang's blood vessel and cut off DNA. Then, the system stops.", "How long do we have till we get to the control tower?", "Up to 10 minutes." "How about the shortest?", "Four."

The three of them got on Huiwon's car. All the children came out to say good bye. Hyunsoo could tell Huiwon was watching them, also. Dr. Chang was too excited to think about children while he was gone. They would be okay without him. It was better that way.

10 The New Beginning

Huiwon flipped the mode to automatic. "I will unlock these doors when your dad swallows the yellow. So until then, stay in the car," Huiwon said. "It is an A-11, stupid woman." Dr. Chang murmured. A-11 and S-09 were too complicated for Hyunsoo and Huiwon to remember. They just called them 'the yellow' and 'the red', whether Dr. Chang liked it or not. The car stayed up in the air. Hyunsoo and Dr. Chang stayed as low as they could in the car to prevent detection. She took the remote so that she could control the vehicle from inside. Hyunsoo watched her disappearing into the dark aisle.

She walked in her own elegant way. She had an unreadable face. She walked passed labs where Q6 was suffering through the transformation to hybrid. Her face was so calm and peaceful that the participants' painful faces looked surreal. She walked into Section A. It was the place where she saw Phin for the first time. Phin was reviewing the participants' files.

"I feel sorry," Huiwon said. "They volunteered." Phin was still looking at the file and answered. "I meant you. You've never thought that you could choose something else." She inserted A-11 to the computer. The yellow local anesthetic dissolved into the system quickly. "What are you doing?", "I am giving you a chance." The conveyer belt stopped and the doors of each section flew open. Newly arrived Q6 didn't have any idea what was going on, but those who were being experimented on knew they had a chance to escape. They all came out from the labs and dashed to exit. "What have you done?" Phin tried to regain control, but nothing worked. Phin slapped Huiwon and she fell on the ground. She smiled. "What would Father do?" Phin was in a panic.

***

Hyunsoo and Dr. Chang were waiting in Huiwon's car. Dr. Chang took out a small bottle of brandy. "Do you really have to drink now?", "Life is too short, kid. I do as

10 The New Beginning

I please." Hyunsoo attempted to take brandy from Dr. Chang and Dr. Chang twisted Hyunsoo's arm to stop him. Hyunsoo squeezed Dr. Chang's neck with his legs. Dr. Chang screamed and stretched his arm to save his brandy. "Be quiet!" Hyunsoo shouted. As Dr. Chang pushed himself toward the window to hurt Hyunsoo, the car flipped and the door flew opened. Hyunsoo, Dr. Chang, and his little brandy fell off on the floor. They were both stupefied. Hyunsoo held his breath. He moved his eyes to check the glass, floor, air, and all sensors of the computer. He couldn't find out if Huiwon opened the door or the door opened itself. His instinct told him she did it.

Dr. Chang was licking his brandy that spilled out on the floor. He was like anybody else who became a slave to their desires. For him, it happened to be alcohol. Hyunsoo didn't have hard feelings toward him anymore. "Let's go, we have a job to do."

Everyone else was heading toward exits except Hyunsoo and Dr. Chang. Going in the opposite direction wasn't easy. They got seperated. "See you at the control tower," Hyunsoo shouted. Dr. Chang knew exactly where he wanted to be. He went to Section M, where mother cells and samples were kept. He inserted a black bottle to the computer. "Wake up, my friend. It's been a while."

In the control tower, there were thousands of monitors. They were showing every corner of Vector, Inc. Hyunsoo took a few steps back. Among the monitors was the father's pale face. All monitors were linked to him through vessels. It was hard to tell which parts were father and computer. Hyunsoo touched the vessels. It felt like a machine. On the other hand, it was soft. There was life to it. He looked at father's face carefully. He could tell A-11 was working. It was time for him to inject the red, S-09. Hyunsoo followed one of the vessels trying to find a port to insert it.

Then, Hyunsoo felt a jolt of electricity shock his hand while holding a vessel. Several cables came out and snaked themselves through Hyunsoo's body. Once they reached his heart, the shock spread quickly. They dominated his body, and Hyunsoo saw father, looking at him. Father was awake.

10 The New Beginning

***

Dr. Chang looked around Section M. The section was well organized. "Like father like son." He felt something behind him. He could tell what it was. He turned around and there was Taurus. Taurus' skin had been peeled off and its hair was thinning. Taurus wasn't in good condition. But still, it knew exactly what it wanted. Taurus wanted its creator. Dr. Chang stroked Taurus's forehead. Dr. Chang shook his hand. It wasn't from the brandy he drank earlier but from fear.

"Good boy," Taurus was listening to his voice. "You managed to survive. You should consider yourself lucky. Your brother, Bo, is a real mess, you know." Dr. Chang stroked Taurus with confidence this time. He extended his other arm to reach the acid. Taurus felt Dr.Chang's fear and hatred from his touch. Dr. Chang threw the acid and doused Taurus's back. Taurus whipped its horn and cut Dr. Chang's flesh. Dr. Chang crawled into a corner and hid. Taurus enjoyed the tension of fear it created. As Taurus was ready for the last attack Dr. Chang closed his eyes.

***

Dark angry eyes were looking at Hyunsoo. Electricity flew throughout Hyunsoo's body. His father was looking for the reason and purpose of his visit. His father, Dr. Kang, traced where he had been and what he had done.

"There isn't a perfect creature, Dad. Why can't you see that after all the experiments?", "It's possible under perfect condition.", "Why can't you face the reality that you can't control life perfectly? Your experiment is proving it and is creating innocent victims.", "The only innocent victim was your mother and she was more than we could afford to lose." The lives Hyunsoo called victims were something to terminate for Dr. Kang. They disgusted him. They are the possible threat to Shubble from Dr. Kang's point of view. "It was Bo who killed mother, not you. Nobody knew he was going to evolve in that way. Even he didn't know." Hyunsoo drove him mad. Dr. Kang thought Hyunsoo was immature and naive.

"The only way to prevent the same crime is to control everything.", "You may be able to control the city, but you don't have the right to control people's lives. And you aren't

10 The New Beginning

capable of it. Please let them go. They will find a way.", "Your happiness has relied on my control. Watch carefully." Dr. Kang's vessel stretched out from the control tower to Shubble. The intensified anger made new vessels and they broke through from the computer and attacked Phin, Huiwon, participants, and citizens. They stretched out further and reached District H. Hybrids ran away from them, but the vessels whipped around and tied them up. The vessels continued to grow and spread to District L. Children couldn't resist the sudden attack. Children felt pain tearing them apart and their lives began fading.

Hyunsoo felt a burning sensation inside. It was Dr. Kang's anger and electricity. Through his father, he could see what Father saw. He could read the pain of each individual in Shubble, District H, and L. He got S-09 and bit it. He broke the glass and swallowed. As Hyunsoo's body absorbed S-09, capsules from the red spread into his vessels and enzymes inside of them became active. With the electricity and the heat, enzymes actively cut off Dr. Kang's DNA. The computers and machines which were part of Dr.Kang sparked and pounded. Hyunsoo focused on letting it flow through the father's system. It reached the others his father attacked and unchained their DNA, too. His blood flow slowed as it went further away. He tried to reach as far as the last person of District L, Hakko. Hyunsoo screamed and struggled to reach his last drop to Hakko. But his effort failed to reach the bright boy.

"Hakko," Hakko thought he heard something among the pain. It was Hyunsoo's voice. "I know it is unbearably painful. I feel it too. But trust me. And give me a chance. Give all of us a chance to start over." Hakko walked closer to the vessels fighting against the pain. The vessels dug into his body. Hyunsoo's last drop of blood finally reached to Hakko.

Hyunsoo absorbed his father's anger and separated each person from the father's vessels, from the system. During the separation, their pieces of DNA were paralyzed and were randomly put together. Hyunsoo couldn't cope with the intensity of his own energy and bounced off from his father and lost consciousness.

"The levels are cleared!" The citizens cheered with joy.

Some hybrids ran through to Shubble and some citizens went over to District H. District L had been found by both citizens and hybrids. They were surprised by the prosperity of the land and poverty of the children.

Huiwon ran to the control tower. Hyunsoo was lying in the middle of the blown off monitors and torn apart vessels. She held him up. "Wake up, Hyunsoo." She never looked so desperate. She frantically shook him, but she couldn't find any strength on his body. She pounded on his chest. "Wake up..." Hope faded from her face. "Please, wake up. I love you." Her voice changed into a cry. She buried her face in his arms. "Ditto." Hyunsoo looked in her eyes and winked.

Lightning Source UK Ltd.
Milton Keynes UK
UKHW040853160920
370003UK00001B/130